BEST FRIENDS FOREVER

Best Friends Forever

SERIES 1

Anna-liese Prince

Icons Media Publishing

ICONS MEDIA PUBLISHING

Contents

About The Author

My name is Anna-Liese Prince, and I am more than just another author. Born on March 14th, 2011, at 1:15 in the afternoon, weighing a mere 6 lbs. 4 oz., my body was small but my ambition was grand. I had two poetry collections under my belt, so when I decided to take up the challenge of writing a fantasy novel, I knew it would be a huge shift in genre – and so began what would prove to be an arduous and tumultuous adventure. Keeping track of it all in a mini diary helped me to stay organized and focused as I worked through the details from concept to computer. Writing took longer than expected due to taking a temporary hiatus to work on another book - Dear Future Anna - adding yet another layer of complexity that required will power and courage to push through.

Taking this roller coaster ride of creation with Best Friend Forever was worth every bump, detour and delay - for if I had known then what I did now, it wouldn't have been nearly as exciting or rewarding.

Love Always,
Annaliese-Prince

Dedication

I owe a debt of gratitude to my mother, without whom this book would not have come into being. Our two-year journey was arduous, filled with long hours and obstacles that could only be overcome by her unwavering encouragement. Through the fog of doubt and writer's block, she shone as a beacon of hope and light. I now proudly look back upon our collaborative efforts at the accomplishment of Best Friends Forever, a milestone in my young writing career. Without her loving support, none of my three prior books (Written with Love and Dear Future Anna) or this one could have seen the light of day. My mother's invaluable guidance helped me break out of my comfort zone, allowing me to explore new heights of creativity. The path I have taken so far has been made easier by the presence of others whose help has served to improve my writing.

My childhood friend Nandita plays a major role in my book. We were very close during Primary school and her character is part of Mandy's circle of best friends. My mother and I captured Nandita's personality perfectly by depicting her as the spontaneous and inquisitive one in the group, even with all she had gone through. In many ways, Nandita is still my best friend today and it was wonderful being able to showcase that in the novel.

Prologue

Earl remained sat on the end of the bed about to speak, but he didn't. His wife had skipped out of the back door about an hour before and now she was back, smiling from ear to ear, raring to go. He was thinking about what she had just said. He knew that this was a part of her brilliant plan, she just wanted money, and that was all. But it was different this time. She wasn't asking for her usual cash flow to continue with her entrepreneurial aspirations; she was suggesting they retire early from their life of crime. They were getting too old for the life that they were living. Whereas Earl used to love certain aspects of it, like the thrill and adrenaline rush, there came a point when it wasn't enough anymore. And he knew he wouldn't be on this earth forever.

"You're right, it's time." Said Earl in a soft tone, looking into his mischievous wife's eyes.

They then hugged each other with Mandy's grandmother revealing a big smile on her face. She had finally achieved what she wanted after years of hard work and dedication.

One

═══════════

The Graveyard

It was a bright and sunny summers day. The sun was gleaming through the little clouds that was left in the sky, warming up the open air and the people below. Children ran around in their beautiful summer dresses and shorts; the fields were divaricating with luscious vegetation. As they ran through the fields, they could feel the radiation of the sun kissing their skin and the humidity growing as the day went on. The congested streets were crowded with buses and taxis, noisy buildings making them seem dangerous. However, new buildings only brought more beautiful views, which must be appreciated whenever it is possible while enjoying old architecture. There can be many social gatherings because jobs are significantly overcrowded by supermarkets and hospitals, so workaholics often sleep late at night and wake up early morning to go to their job sites.

The aroma of donuts and confectioneries permeated the city as freshly cooked treats from the bakeries were made for people to eat. This cycle was changed as people were energized and joyous, having a great sleep and feeling enthused about the day as sunlight shone through their curtains into their dismal rooms. Who wouldn't be happy for a few weeks with no weather changes? The vegetation flourished into captivating blooms, and trees grew into impenetrable forests.

As the citizens of the city gradually became distressed, they reversed their ignorant remarks towards unhappy humans, becoming those very people themselves. In the morning, they walked around with umbrellas on the streets and at night when the sun's rays diminished and the moon shone, darkness illuminated buildings, towns, and even the entire world, cooling everyone down with contentment.

On this particular day, a young girl called Mandy Allard was in a graveyard searching for her dead parents' grave. She loved reading the epitaphs on each headstone, and she often laughed at them as though they were caricatures from a particularly imaginative cartoonist. Today, however, she could not laugh. A cold wind blew over her hair and knitted jacket; her cheeks felt chapped against the sunless sky. She held back tears as she looked for them, hoping to mourn the loss of her loved ones in their final resting place. As she brushed away fallen leaves and weeds from their tombstone, Mandy saw another child's tombstone. Wondering why a child would be buried here- perhaps someone lost or killed in a car crash- Mandy wondered if it was her fault that the young girl had died, as she felt that everything that went wrong in life was her fault. As she examined the stone, she realized that although there was only one date carved out upon the stone, with no month or year listed afterward, she knew that something was very wrong here.

As Mandy approached the grave of a young girl, she was fascinated by the information that was written there. She started to circle around it, examining every aspect and wanting to learn more about this unknown person. She became so invested in studying the other grave, she forgot why she had come to the cemetery in the first place. Suddenly, a voice filled with frustration rang out from nearby, breaking her concentration and reminding her of her purpose.

"GET OVER HERE NOW YOU BRAT!" yelled a voice that Mandy recognized well.

"No, grandmother. I just want to visit my parents' grave," she replied with some sass.

"I haven't been able to yet because of the um.... darkness." The older woman sighed with annoyance.

"You have a few minutes before I'm ready to leave," she said gruffly. Without missing a beat, Mandy took off running towards her parents' gravesite.

"I wish she would stop calling me a brat," Mandy complained under her breath as she ran.

Mandy slowly made her way to her parents' graves and sat down between them, cleaning the dirt from the headstones before setting some flowers in the pots near their graves. She spoke with them as if they were still alive, recounting how hard things had been since they passed away.

"Hey mum and dad, I hope you're doing well. I've really missed you both so much. Gran's still being nasty - always scolding me and hitting me. I wish you were here; why did you have to go? I know Gran was involved in your death somehow, but I can't prove it. If I ask the police for help, they'll take me into care, and that would be awful. But if I stay strong and brave like you always told me too, I'll make it out okay until then. That's what our family motto was, remember? 'Be brave and never cave.' I'm so looking forward to seeing you again one day - alive and with me. I love you both so much."

Tears streamed down Mandy's face as she continued talking to her parents. Despite loving coming to visit them, she could never stop herself from crying.

"I know mum, you hated to see me cry," she said apologetically.

The mention of Katie's grave suddenly reminded Mandy of her investigation into the girl's disappearance from her tombstone inscription; she wanted to find out who had removed the words with such a disrespectful act.

After paying her respects to her parents at their graves, Mandy decided on the spur of the moment to go and visit Katie's grave. When she got there, she noticed something strange. The 'K' in Katie's name had been removed from the tombstone. There was also a picture of what looked like one of her old friends with the same name. As she mulled this over, Mandy noticed that Katie's grave had been dug up and the casket was missing! Who could have taken it? And why?

Mandy didn't know why she cared so much about Katie's grave, but in her heart, she knew there was a reason. Suddenly, she felt a cold hand touch her shoulder and spun around in fright. Was it a kidnapper? Her grandmother playing pranks? Or had her parents come back from the dead to take revenge on her for caring more about an unknown stranger than them?

Oh, sweet Jesus, thought Mandy with fear. Her legs shook and her heart thudded against her chest. When she turned around, she saw a lovely young girl. The girl's blue eyes were more beautiful than the deepest part of the sea, and her hair was golden and captivating - it seemed to give off its own light. Her skin was radiant, like the clouds in the sky - if you touched it, it would feel soft like cotton candy. She had tiny orange freckles on her nose that looked like butterflies. She wore a white dress with butterflies and hearts all over it, as if it had been made for her in particular. Her shoes were also white. As Mandy looked at her from head to toe, she saw that the girl stood on two feet, making her seem even more real to Mandy. As their eyes met, the young girl gave Mandy a friendly smile – one that seemed meant to comfort her and put her at ease. Mandy responded with a big grin of her own.

"Greetings, Mandy." The young girl spoke softly, catching the attention of the startled girl.

Mandy was taken aback that this person knew her name.

"Um, hello there." She said uneasily, scanning her eyes around nervously. "Who are you and how did you know my name?" she asked.

"I'm not sure why I know your name, I'm not sure why I remember anything at this point actually, maybe we went to school together," responded Katy.

"Wait a second...Are you the young girl from the photograph? There's no way you could be alive," Mandy replied hastily.

"Now hold on one minute, wait...you do look an awful lot like the girl who went missing a few years back. She was close to your age and her parents have been extremely distraught ever since she disappeared; plus your name is exactly the same as hers, it has to be a coincidence. You aren't even dead!" exclaimed Mandy in surprise.

"Yes, my name is Katie and I don't know what happened to me or where I'm from. All I remember is waking up in the grave and I definitely don't want to go back there!" declared Katie.

"Oh my gracious! That is very strange." said Mandy in awe.

"Any way, I must be off; if I don't meet up with my grandmother soon she may grow very upset."

A desperate grin spread across Katie's face. "I was scared to find out what happened to me until this morning, but now I don't need the full memory back to know that I am supposed to be with you. If we keep looking for answers, maybe we can get them."

Her blue eyes were pleading. She grabbed Mandy's hand and squeezed it in her own. The sparkles from earlier glittered on her cheekbones as she fluttered her eyelashes at Mandy. "Please come with me, I don't want to search alone anymore. Since I held your hand today, I feel like I have known you forever. There is something going on here and only you can help me figure it out. Please please please help me!"

Mandy shivered all over seeing the eager look in Katie's face, the hint of a smile tugging at the corner of her mouth, and the wings brushing against her arm. She wondered why this incredibly beautiful girl would want anything more than friendship from her. Filled with a sense of dread and destiny combined, she nodded solemnly, agreeing to help Katie.

The two girls heard Mandy's grandmother hollering as

she approached them. Katie was instantly taken aback by the old woman in front of her; there was something that made her feel uneasy, uncomfortable and scared. The woman looks like a crone out of a fairy tale, with long grey hair and a ragged dress. She wears a red shawl that covers a hunched back and a gnarled walking stick. She looks like she has seen centuries pass by and seen them well. Her face bears a strong resemblance to Mandy's, but the eyes are dark like coal in a blacksmith's forge. Her eyes were crooked and small, like pin-pricks of black-brown that made you want to look away. Her hair was a brittle grey, like straw in the wind. Running her fingers through it, she noticed it was greasy and dishevelled, nothing like anyone she had seen before. Her face was thin and colourless, the face of an old woman. Her body was large and round, with an odour of mothballs and wet earth.

Katie's face was filled with revulsion. "I told you not to be late, Mandy! Where have you been?" yelled Grandma.

"I was speaking with my parents; I apologize for being late," Mandy replied meekly.

"Your apology isn't enough. You should be thankful that I even let you go visit those useless people. They were nothing when they were alive, and they are nothing now. Wait until we get back home; I cannot tolerate this casual attitude of yours anymore." Her grandmother grabbed Mandy by the ears and pulled her away as Katie stood incredulous at the disrespect she was witnessing. She couldn't follow them, so all she could do was watch helplessly as her friend was dragged off. The last thing Mandy saw was Katie's shocked face looking back at her.

Two

The Basement

"I'm so sorry Grandma, I didn't see the time... I've been trying to go and see Mum and Dad... or at least pay my respects, but it's just so difficult with my guilt." Mandy said through a tear-stained face as she hung her head down in shame.

"Sorry doesn't do anything for me does it?" growled the old woman as she clenched her fists.

She pulled Mandy's hair directly from her scalp and threw her into the basement. The young woman fell down the steps and onto the basement ground. She then tried to quickly stand up before her grandmother had felt the opportunity to rush down the stairs and hit her again, she quickly stood up and pleaded for mercy.

"No, please! I don't want to be in here!" Mandy begged.

"Well life isn't always fair, is it? And do you really think those crocodile tears are going to work like they did for your mother? Well it isn't, now, you can stay down in this dirty, smelly place all night, if that's how you feel about things. Let me tell you something dearie, if you don't change your attitude, it will only get worse from here on out." Said Mandy's grandmother with an evil grin on her lips as she closed the door leaving Mandy in complete darkness.

Starvation and thirst were almost a new normal, and Mandy knew she could survive on half a litre of water and two slices of bread for a couple days before her body started to shut down, but she was not given anything to eat. She navigated herself around the basement, trying not to touch any rusty or dirty things because of the germs and contamination. In one corner she found the old blanket that she slept with on the first night that she was trapped in her grandma's house, as well as the lamp that had gone unused since then. She tried to get as comfortable as she could, for which she didn't succeed, and slowly cried herself to sleep on the cold hard floor.

Three

We Meet Again

It was nearly 12 o'clock in the morning, and Mandy lay on the freezing basement floor. The colourful blanket around her was stained and tattered; she was cold and hungry. She had grown accustomed to her grandmother's neglectful behaviour and hoped that tonight wouldn't be different. As she shifted her position, she heard a creak as the top of the stairs opened - her grandmother had risen. In fear, Mandy shut her eyes tightly but kept one open slightly to see what would happen next. To her relief, it was not her grandmother who stepped into the room, but her beloved grandfather Earl, carrying a plate of food in his hands. He knelt next to Mandy and tenderly kissed her forehead before pushing back some wayward strands of hair from her face.

As he stood up again, he murmured words of love that echoed in Mandy's mind without needing any response:

"I love you too grandad". Without making another sound, Earl left as quietly as he entered. Instead of feeling anger at being neglected once more, Mandy was grateful for her grandfather's thoughtfulness and love; she revelled in the knowledge that he cared enough about her to risk his wife's wrath by bringing food down into the basement.

Mandy then sat up on the ground to eat, wrapping herself in the sheets, her cumbersome movements made it clear that she was not very used to being sick. She started to take a bite of food bit by bit, and as she did so her distress at being sick remained visible on her face. A cold and firm hand touched her shoulder.

A shiver ran down her spine. She turned around slowly. In the monstrously large basement which had only one window, with only three little lamps attached to the wall, she could see nothing but the shadows dancing on the walls behind Katie's figure. And Katie was standing there looking at her concern etched on her face.

Mandy reached out and touched Katie's hand before saying

"Are you real?"

"Yes, how did you know it was me?" asked Katie as if offended by a question, or rather perhaps by Mandy's very doubt that she was there.

"I just had a feeling, that is all…and I thought you left?" said Mandy.

Katie leaned against the wall and stared outside through the dirty basement window which was covered in old flies nests and dirt blown up from the street by cars passing by. The uncut grass out front looked like an overgrown lawn after two months without mowing; in fact, it felt like no one had set foot in this garden for years since Mandy had been taken away from home to live with her grandparents.

Katie peered out the window, a look of concern on her face as she asked Mandy,

"Where are your parents? How come they're treating you like this?" Mandy rested her head against the wall and remembered the day she had lost them.

"I sat in my mother's silver Volvo as it hummed down the bumpy dirt road," Mandy said.

"The tunnel was getting darker when we drove out into the sunshine."

She took a deep breath and continued.

"Mom leaned over to kiss me on the cheek and I saw her diamond earring sparkle in the sun. As soon as we drove onto Grandma's property Mom sat up and grew tenser. Grandma opened our car door and whispered something strange sounding to Mom. After dinner I wandered around. All of a sudden, my parents started to become faint and weak before they finally passed away. My grandmother scurried around them and quickly ushered me into my bedroom so that I couldn't see what was happening. I screamed for my parents, but they never responded back."

Mandy remembered that the woman had threatened to find any information she had about that night and destroy it, along with the severe punishment she would get. Katie knew something was off with that woman. She suggested they both go off and investigate what really happened to Mandy's parents and Katie herself.

"Where are we going?" asked Mandy.

"We're going to figure out what happened," replied Katie.

Mandy laughed,

"But how? I'm stuck in this basement."

"Well, how ironic," said Katie, flashing a smile.

"I'm dead. I have the ability to help you escape."

Mandy was taken aback but wanted to take this chance for freedom. She hesitantly asked, "Okay, so what do I have to do?"

"Well, if we want to succeed, we need to sneak around without looking suspicious or getting caught."

Mandy excitedly agreed, but then stopped herself suddenly.

"Wait, what if my grandparents come here and don't find me? What will happen then?"

"Don't be afraid, I've got this completely under control," explained Katie, as she grabbed the pillows from the other side of the room and placed them beneath Mandy's sheets. "They may be a little dirty, but your grandparents are old enough not to take notice. Now, grab my hand tightly, we're going to walk through this wall together," said Katie.

"Wait...what!" exclaimed Mandy in shock.

"You do realize I'm human, right? A very big-headed human whose head will definitely crack open if this doesn't work out, leaving me dead!"

Mandy was scared but Katie tried to assuage her fears, saying,

"Please don't worry. You'll have to trust me – it won't hurt you; I promise. You know I would never put you in danger, correct? I've done this many times before so I know I can get us through the wall safely. Okay?"

"Okay then. If you think you can make it happen, let's do it!" Mandy stated confidently.

Holding hands tightly, Mandy closed her eyes tightly for what she anticipated would be a tremendous jolt and suddenly they were gone from the dusty old room.

Four

―――――――――

The Silent Cries

Earl stared at the dark ceiling while his wife let out a guttural gurgle in her sleep. Some days he felt like she was more of a sister to him than a mate. Gently, he pushed his sleeping body aside and lowered himself from the bed onto the floor. He grabbed his robe from the edge of the bed and placed it on before slipping his feet into his slippers. Silent as a mouse, Earl padded down the hall to the kitchen, though not to get food. With one hand on the wall to steady himself and another holding his dinner plate, he passed through the living room and stepped outside. The moist air oozed over him, soothing his head like cool water poured over heated skin. There were two things that Earl hated: hearing Karen's snores echo off of every surface of their home and being cooped up inside all day. He preferred when everyone was asleep, especially now that he had something to hide.

Holding his plate of dinner, Mandy's grandfather made his way down the back stairs of his house to a metal door. He opened it and stepped inside, flipping on the hallway lights as he passed closed doors. Taking out a set of keys, he searched for the right one to unlock the last door in this room. Realizing he couldn't juggle both the plate and keys at the same time, he placed the plate on the ground again and soon found the key. Muttering to himself how old age was getting to him, Mandy's grandfather unlocked the door. With a flick of a switch, it became apparent that there was a prison cell on the right side of the room with faint cries coming from within. Ignoring these cries, he threw a plate full of food into it along with some cutlery.

Making his way to the sink, Mandy's grandfather grabbed a black bucket and placed it beneath the faucet. He ran both hot and cold water until the bucket was filled. Taking up a metal bar he set the bucket on the ground, then lugged it over to the cell. His gaze was unwavering as he looked upon the small figure within.

"Please," came a plea from inside its confines, but was ignored by Mandy's grandfather. He rose and shut the cell door. Leaving the room, he closed the heavy doors behind him and paused for a moment outside, beaming with satisfaction. "How beautiful," he murmured before walking away.

Five

The Arrival

K atie transported them into an unknown realm, much to Mandy's surprise.

"Where are we? You didn't tell me you could do this!" Mandy exclaimed.

"Hehe! I guess I forgot to mention it!" Katie said with a giggle before pausing. Mandy fixed her with a disapproving stare as she continued.

"My abilities are stronger when in the presence of a human soul, especially children. This is where deceased souls go to understand why they're here and some leave in order to comprehend more. Some just stay here and remain stuck in their hurt and sadness from what someone may have done to them, such as myself..." She gestured around the afterlife as they walked through it.

"In the afterlife, once your soul is free of its bindings, we no longer appear as we did in life; everyone becomes one, devoid of blood and bone.", Katie said.

Mandy laughed at this thought. "Ahh, so we'll be like walking lumps of unseasoned meat then? Gotcha!"

As Mandy's eyes scanned the area, she gaped in astonishment at the bright sunlight reflected onto the sidewalks; like a golden hammer striking a blacksmith, they gleamed with the light of the sun.

A place that Mandy can't describe, a place that is indescribable, a realm that is outside of her knowledge. Her eyes see the landscape, but her mind cannot understand it, her mind cannot comprehend it. She sees a town square littered with the bones of the dead who have yet to move on to the afterlife. Here they walk among each other, but they do not speak, they do not interact with one another.

The people here were bone, framed with skin and muscle. They walked in their skeleton form: the whole, top and bottom, cranium included.

The area smelled of burnt wood and something else, a scent that Mandy couldn't identify. An odour of dead and decaying lingered in the air, like a rotting corpse.

The air here stank like a landfill, with a mild sweat smell, like the inside of a gym. Mandy wrinkled her nose to avoid the odour.

As they arrived at the desolated area, they stepped into a quiet and gloomy home. A grey-haired old man stood in the doorway, his walking stick in hand, grinning warmly as Katie walked in.

"Ahhhh! Where have you been, my darling? I was so worried about you" he said, reaching out to hug her.

"Grandpa, I brought us a guest, she'll be staying with us tonight," Katie replied. "This is Mandy."

Mandy smiled. "Pleased to meet you, sir.

"What brings you to Ghost Town today Mandy? Better yet, how did such a pretty girl die so young?" Asked Grandpa.

Katie spoke up then.

"That's why we're here grandad, she isn't...er...how can I put this? She isn't dead yet. She's helping me figure things out."

Her grandfather gasped. "Not dead yet? With blood still running through her veins? Is that what you said?"

Katie nodded as she looked down bashfully.

"Yes grandad, she's still a human being. Blood and all."

"Are you crazy, my child? What on Earth prompted you to do something like this--to come to this abandoned town? You know that if that clock hits a certain time, she will never be able to return to the world of the living," explained Granddad.

"Yes, I understand Grandpa, but hear me out," responded Katie.

Mandy then interjected as she sat up from the couch.

"Whoa, wait a sec, let me make sure I'm understanding this," said Mandy.

" So you mean to tell me that you knew that if I did not get back home in time, I'd be gone for good? And you didn't tell me?" She asked incredulously.

"I'm so sorry! I thought that if I told you, you wouldn't help me. I was panicked and I get that it looks bad, but it wasn't my intention," said Katie apologetically.

Mandy paused for a moment and put her right hand on her head in contemplation.

"This is bad...this is really very bad. Friends don't do this to each other. I trusted you, Katie." Tears welled up in Mandy's eyes.

"I'm incredibly sorry, please forgive me," said Katie remorsefully.

"Listen--I don't want to die yet, and I won't let it happen. So whatever we need to do, let's get going." Mandy said determinedly.

"Agreed," replied Katie.

"And no more lies--friends support each other and look out for each other." A small smile broke through Mandy's tears as she spoke.

"I've never had a friend like you Mandy...and again, I am terribly sorry..."Katie stated humbly.

"How delightful," said the elderly man with a grin, "but while you two are here being so lovable, the spirits have already taken over Mandy's soul."

Mandy replied in shock,

"Wait, what?"

"Yes my dear, and Katie, your name has been erased from the living world. When I arrived at the cemetery your name was on the tombstone, but a few minutes later most of it had vanished—your picture and date of birth were gone as well. It's quite strange if you ask me," Katie commented.

"What do you mean?" asked Mandy.

"Unfortunately, Katie has been gone for a long time because her soul hasn't been laid to rest. If her name is erased from her tombstone then it will be like she never existed, or never even came into this world. Her parents, friends and family won't remember that she ever existed. We should figure out why and how this happened." Grandad suggested.

Katie sadly replied, "but that's the problem grandad, I don't know—I just can't remember."

Grandpa tried to steady himself on his walking stick before he said,

"Let's take a moment to think about the day you died. But before we do that, shall I make us some tea?" Said Grandpa as he walked into the kitchen.

Katie then smiled and responded, "that would be great grandpa, thank you."

Mandy asked, "So let's think. Do you remember where you were the morning you died? What were you wearing? Or better yet, where were you headed?"

Katie replied, "I'm not quite sure, but I do remember that my mother made a very pretty dress for me--the prettiest I'd ever seen in my life. It was a long white dress with butterflies and hearts on it. My mom was a dressmaker; she could make me any beautiful outfit I could imagine. It always made me feel so special."

"So, you were wearing a very long, white dress with distinctive butterflies and hearts on it?"

"Yes," Katie said.

Mandy looked at her in surprise. "Is this the same dress you're wearing right now?"

Katie looked down at her attire and answered, "Yes, I guess it is. I didn't realize until just now."

"Maybe being a ghost makes you a little slow," Mandy joked.

"Nope," Katie laughed, "I've been slow since birth; it runs in my family!"

They both laughed before getting serious again.

"Okay, so your mother's amazing and she made this beautiful dress for you that you're wearing right now—is that right?"

Katie nodded in agreement.

"Yes," Katie replied.

"But this dress is stunning. Where were you going?" Mandy asked with curiosity in her voice.

"I'm not sure, but I do remember my father was away on a business trip and my mother was very upset. She was on the phone arguing about something - saying 'you always do this, it's an important day for your child and you will miss it again". Said Katie.

"Hmmm, I see," pondered Mandy. "Maybe you had to attend some sort of gathering like a dinner or lunch? You used to enjoy stuffing your face."

"A dinner? I can't recall what kind of dinner it was," said Katie.

"Who did your family have close ties with? Did you have any close friends or relatives that may have hosted it?" asked Mandy.

"Well, yes, we used to have people over to our house quite frequently because my parents were quite wealthy. We would host these extravagant parties and everyone from the family would come together and eat."

Mandy responded with interest, "That's very interesting." She then asked, "So while you were younger, where did you kids usually play?"

Katie replied, "We would run around the house; there wasn't much supervision. I was really close to my cousin though. We did everything together—ate the same food, wore matching clothes—we were like twins."

Mandy excitedly suggested, "Maybe your cousin could tell us more about how you went missing!"

Katie agreed, "Yes, that's a great idea!"

Suddenly Katie's grandad appeared with a tray of tea.

"So, how are my little detectives doing? Found anything interesting?" he asked.

Katie and Mandy quickly said their goodbyes and rushed out of the house. As soon as they left, Katie's grandfather sat down and gulped down his cup of tea at once; spilling it all over the floor as he exhaled heavily. He muttered tiredly to himself,

"Guess I'm off to bed then!" before quickly falling asleep in a deep snoring slumber.

Six

———

Nancy's House

I t was two in the morning when Katie and Mandy landed on her cousin's front garden. As she looked around, memories of playing with her cousin were reawakened within Katie. She remembered they had been laughing and running through the garden with their wet hair and bathing suits; then suddenly, her cousin's parents appeared with glasses of lemonade for them to have a break.

"Hey, are you okay?" asked Mandy as she placed a gentle hand on Katie's arm. The girl came back to reality and nodded at Mandy.

"Yes, I'm fine. I recall this place; we used to play here all the time."

Mandy replied, "It seems your memories are coming back

to you. Let's go find out if your cousin can shed some more light on everything."

Katie took hold of Mandy's hands, and they were instantly transported into her cousin's room. When they arrived, they found her asleep. Hesitant about waking her up, Katie was ready to leave, but Mandy urged her not to give up so quickly.

"Why can't you wake her up?" Mandy inquired.

"She won't be able to feel me," Katie responded.

Katie placed a hand on Mandy's shoulder and whispered in her ear. "I don't fully understand it yet, but you're a full human, so she'll be able to sense you better than me."

Mandy nodded and approached the pink bed where Nancy lay asleep. The bed was massive, probably queen-sized, covered in pink and yellow flowers and adorned with colourful lights. Mandy tried to rouse Nancy gently, but it wasn't working.

"She's a deep sleeper like our granddad," Katie said. "You might have to give her a hard punch in the head or something."

Mandy rolled her eyes. "I'm not going to punch her in the head Katie are you crazy?"

"What was her name again?" she asked.

"Nancy," Katie responded.

"Hello there, Nancy," Mandy said quietly as she leaned over the bed.

"Can you wake up for me, please? I need to ask you some questions before I go." She chuckled softly at the end.

Nancy stirred slightly and rolled over onto her stomach, not fully awake yet.

"Hey lady!" Mandy prodded her unintentionally as Nancy fell off the bed and hit the ground with a thud. Suddenly awake and confused, Nancy looked around the room, she sat up on the floor, clutching her head and groaning in pain. The light is blinding in its green colour, like being in the deepest darkest jungle at noon.

Nancy's room was covered in stuffed animals and colourful lights, it was a beautiful girly room, almost made for a princess. She begins to rub her eyes and see's Mandy standing before her. A stranger, she thinks. now realising that there was a stranger in her room Nancy let out a loud scream.

"Who the hell are you?" she yelled at Mandy. Mandy hears a ringing in her ears as if she's been screaming at full volume for hours. She hears a high-pitched squeal like a kettle ready to burst.

Nancy begins to feel her head for bumps and scrapes, no doubt a result from falling off the bed.

Nancy's screams were so loud that her voice cracked and she started to cry as she clambered to her feet. "Get out of my room right now!" shouted Nancy.

"Please, stop shouting, I can explain," said Mandy as she attempted to placate Nancy. "Are you here to kidnap me?" asked Nancy. "Absolutely not! My name is Mandy and I'm a friend of Katie's. She sent me here to ask you some questions."

Nancy was clearly unconvinced. "That's a huge lie! How could she have possibly sent you? What are you talking about?"

Mandy assured her that she wasn't lying and repeated her assertion that Katie was in the room, but Nancy wasn't buying it. "Stop playing with my emotions! Katie has been missing for years and now you come into my room spewing lies!"

Nancy rushed towards the phone on her bedside table, threatening to call the police, but Mandy managed to grab it and throw it out of the open window. Desperate to be believed, Katie shouted from across the room: "Wait – tell her that you know she has a birthmark behind her ears!"

Mandy quickly complied. "Yes, I know you have a birthmark behind your ears," she stated.

"What? Who told you that?" Nancy exclaimed as she stood on her bed.

"Katie told me, she is right here with us now," Mandy said.

"No, you're lying" Nancy replied. "Everyone knows I have a birthmark behind my ears, as a matter of fact you could have seen it when you tried to wake me up. You impostor!"

"Impostor, oh hell no, you did not just call me an imposter! Bring it on melon head!" Mandy shouted as she tried to fight Nancy. Katie then grabbed her arms and pulled her aside.

"Calm down Bugs Bunny, she's scared. We have to find a way to convince her that I am indeed here." Katie then paused for a moment to think.

"Tell her I still remember that she liked Malcom and wouldn't let anyone near him except me," Katie said.

Mandy then relayed the information to Nancy.

"She remembers that you had a big crush on Malcom and wouldn't allow anyone near him, because you trusted only her."

Nancy's face began to relax a little.

"How did you know that?" she asked Mandy .

"Tell her I also remember when we used to cuddle under

the covers when we were kids, especially when we heard the thunder and rain," Katie added.

Katie approached Nancy's bed and began to reminisce on their times spent together as children, especially during thunderstorms. Nancy interrupted her with a fond memory.

"Especially when it used to rain and thunder". Nancy slowly sat down on her bed, then questioned Katie's sudden disappearance.

"What had happened to her?" Asked Nancy.

Mandy stepped in to respond. "This is why we are here; we need to know what really happened to Katie the last time you saw her," she said.

Nancy tried to think for a second before being interrupted by someone rushing up the stairs—it was her father! Nancy instructed everyone to hide as she ducked beneath the covers. Her father rushed into the room, looking around the room before walking over to check if Nancy was okay; and apologized for waking her. He followed up with a reassuring promise that he would always be there for her if she ever needed him. Unbeknownst to him, Mandy was barely able to contain a loud fart which burst through the silence.

Mandy exhaled in relief as she hid beneath Nancy's bed. Nancy glanced around, quickly realizing that Mandy had released the funk under her bed – and she had to take the blame for it.

"Oh, excuse me Father," Nancy began, trying to sound casual. "I'm a bit gassy today."

"It must be that milk you drank earlier," he replied. "You know you're lactose intolerant!"

"Yes, I know, Daddy," Nancy responded.

He then snorted, commenting on how putrid her fart was. The smell reached his nose, causing him to stand up and try catching his breath by coughing.

"Jesus Christ, Nancy! What did you eat? The entire cow?!" Somehow managing to stay calm, he bid her goodnight before hastily leaving the room.

Nancy then stood up and Mandy crept out from underneath the bed.

Nancy looked at Mandy in complete shock. "Why did you do that? You almost killed everyone in here!"

Mandy apologized profusely, explaining that she couldn't hold it in any longer. Shaking her head in disbelief, Nancy asked what they were talking about before the incident happened.

"Okay," Mandy continued with a heavy sigh, "so where were we? Right – we need to understand what happened the day you last saw Katie."

The only thing they could recall was that Katie had been wearing an incredibly lovely dress; her mother was a seamstress, and she had made it for her.

"I remember because it was her ninth birthday, everyone from our school attended. Then right when it seemed like all the guests had arrived, this peculiar, wrinkled old man with grey hair and a short beard showed up bearing a gift. He said he was Katie father's friend. We just assumed it was true and carried on with the fun day, but I noticed him staring at Katie in the crowd. At the time I didn't think too much of it - until she went missing."

Nancy reflected as Mandy asked her to explain more about this strange man's behaviour throughout the party and what he looked like.

"He was around 5 feet tall - maybe taller - with long white hair that looked like it hadn't seen a brush in years. He kept to himself, walking cautiously around the room (he tried to blend in). His eyes were dull and full of hunger; they quivered with desire as he observed everything going on around him (as if he were waiting for something special)."

Mandy stared in disbelief as the image of her beloved grandpa flashed through her mind: balding,5 feet tall, with a wild mane of white hair. Her lips quivered and an agonizing scream escaped her throat as she registered what she was hearing: he was a killer, a brute, a predator. Tears pooled in Mandy's eyes and spilled down her cheeks as sobs wracked her body. Katie stepped forward and enveloped her in an embrace as Nancy took some comfort in the gesture and silently mouthed her gratitude. But there was no time to lose; they had to act fast. All three girls' attention was then pulled to the brilliant hues of yellow-and-red that filled the sky.

Seven

The Missing Letters

Anthony slowly made his way through the graveyard, sweeping a path to each grave with a steady hand. When he arrived at Katie's final resting place, his sunken eyes widened in terror. The lettering on her tombstone had been maliciously altered: Half of the letters were missing and an M was added in their place.

Anthony dropped his broom in shock and bolted towards his office, desperation clawing at him like an icy wind. Upon entering, he collapsed into a chair and shut his eyes tightly, a thousand terrible scenarios racing through his mind as he tried to think of how he could fix this thing quickly. He surged up from the chair and grabbed a piece of paper with instructions for the proper lettering. His heart thumping wildly, Anthony sped back to the graveyard, glancing furtively over his shoulder to make sure nobody had seen him.

He anxiously compared the paper to the grave again—only to be met by a deep groan of despair: "Wait! how could this happen again?"

Seeing he was in distress the old man asked him a question,

"What happened?"

The young graveyard worker took a large gulp from his water bottle before mumbling,

"The graveyard...it's gone. The words are strange! I'm going to get fired if you can't help me."

"I told you to be careful with your spells, now tell me what happened!" he said, shaking his head with disappointment.

"It was a girl called Katie something, her grave, ermm – the words had disappeared, this time into a girl named Man something, I don't think her full name has appeared just yet. I don't know what to do! Help me!" The boy looked terrified.

"Oh no...did you create the circle like I taught you? Remember to use salt!" The elder scowled.

"Chant the ghost's name and see what happens. Do you need me to write it down for you?"

"Yes please!" the boy replied in innocence before departing with instructions scribbled on a piece of paper. He kept repeating, it'll all work out...it'll all work out...as he went on his way.

Eight

The Mystery Unfolds

Mandy and Katie had just arrived at Mandy's house in the early hours of the morning. They sat quietly for a moment, catching their breaths. With a sigh, Mandy turned to Katie with sad eyes and noticed that her friend was still trembling.

"Oh Katie, I'm so sorry." Her tone shifted from panicked to understanding as she took in her friends frightened expression.

"But we will get through this together."

Katie looked up to her friend,

"How? How could it be grandad? He isn't like my grandma, why would he do this?" She walked around her bedroom as Katie attempted to soothe her.

"My grandfather has always been so kind to me - he even defended me from my grandmother a few times. Anything I needed when my parents died, he was there for me without fail. There is no way he'd ever do something like this. No matter what, I refuse to believe it!", exclaimed Mandy as she continued to pace.

Katie was about to speak up but then heard a noise coming from downstairs,

"Can you hear that? It sounds...it sounds an awful lot like-"

"Shhh! Listen, can you hear that?" interrupted Mandy as she hastily wiped away her tears.

Mandy and Katie crept up the stairs, each step creaking like a banshee's scream. The muffled cries of her grandparents echoed above her head like thunder, reverberating through her bones.

"This is why I killed them! That girl has to go!" screamed her grandmother. Horrified, Mandy and Katie huddled against the door, fear seeping into their veins as they heard the words uttered from the other side.

"I'm telling you, Earl... I can't put up with this anymore." Her grandmother shouted angrily.

"That little girl has to go! We have worked too hard on our plan for years now, if we get caught, it would be all for nothing," furious determination shone in her grandparent's voices. Mandy scrambled back, her heart pounding in her chest as she tried to comprehend what was going on. The life insurance money? Was this all about money?! Fear and rage boiled up inside of her as she heard her grandparents plotting to take away everything she had left -- no more would she be willing to sit idle while they destroyed her family! she had to leave before they could take away her parents dream of providing a better life for her.

Mandy's grandma spoke up from her seat on the bed,

"It's time for this to end, Earl. We both agreed to take out her parents, and we almost have all the documents in order to get the money. Let's just sell this house and go far away from here."

Earl stayed still on the edge of the bed, considering what his wife had said. He understood it was time: he was growing too old for this life, and he wanted to retire. But it was hard to stop - it had been such a long time - and he didn't know how much longer he would be around.

"I agree," he replied quietly.

The two embraced each other, Mandy's grandmother sporting a wide smile on her face; she had finally achieved what she wanted.

At the top of the stairs, Mandy stood still in shock and bewilderment. It was the first time in her life that she couldn't find any words. Even at her parents' funeral she had managed to craft an amazing speech that left everyone astounded. However, now she felt all alone in the world, without parents or grandparents or friends she could turn to. She never expected that both of them - her own blood - could do something like this.

"Oh, God!" Mandy covered her mouth with one hand and bounded in fits of sobs down the hallway. Her knees buckled under her weight as she reached the end of the hall. She could not hold herself in any longer. The truth was like a gunshot wound: sudden, unexpected, and certain to cause damage. Katie put one arm around Mandy's shoulder and pulled her friend close. She whispered in her ear that everything would be okay.

Nine

The Findings

She absentmindedly sank down onto a hard object without much thought. Then, it all came back to her. Her grandmother had never approved of her mother or father. She was the one who had driven them away and made them start from scratch. Even though they'd become wealthy, she'd still forced her daughter out into the world without protection.

Katie absorbed this information in shock, unable to believe what she was hearing. Her grandmother, the woman she'd loved like family. The same grandmother who had, according to Mandy, driven her parents away out of jealousy? Katie shook off her disbelief as well as something slimy under her bottom that moved and made a noise when she shifted uncomfortably.

Her grandmother was crazy! Someone she used to love. No way! No! This didn't make sense-or did it?

"What's that under your butt?" Katie asked, trying to sound comforting yet curious at the same time.

"I don't know! Who can I trust now? No one will even believe me!" sobbed Mandy.

"Wait, I think there's a lever under you! Do you mind if I-?"

Before either of them could move an inch, a voice yelled out from beneath Mandy's butt:

"Get me out of here! Please help me! Is there anyone there? Don't leave me here to die! Somebody help me."

Mandy's heart hammered against her chest as she screamed for somebody to hang on, they were coming. Her voice quivered with the weight of the chaos that was rampaging inside her. Knowing that someone needed help made them rise, trying to stay composed while still being under the shock of the news. They pulled back the rusty lever carefully, not knowing what lay behind it, only knowing that a child was there somewhere. As the old and dirt-covered stairway appeared, Mandy regretted her decision to help an unknown individual. Doubt crept in, questioning whether Katie would be useful due to her apparent death.

The sound of crying guided them through the darkened

rooms until it became deafeningly loud. Finally, they found its source—a locked cage containing a wretched figure.

"It's probably locked," Katie said hesitantly. Their hearts sank with dread as they approached it - they had not expected to find something so terrible here. When they opened the cage door, a putrid smell overwhelmed their senses, The cell reeked of faeces and urine, it was a putrid smell that made their eyes water and noses burn.

Fear. A metallic taste filled their mouth. It was the taste of terror and pain, an emotion that one person should never have to experience. she was scared and alone, lost in a world of torture. The sight that greeted them was revolting and filled with incarceration; why wasn't it closed? Mandy wondered, unable to comprehend how something so cruel could exist in this world.

The child inside was malnourished and disfigured from days spent trapped in the tiny cell. Tears streamed down their dirt-stained face as they reached out for help. It pained Mandy's heart to see such suffering in one so young.

Katie was the first one to venture inside, thinking to herself, "It won't hurt me if I'm already dead, right?" Mandy followed close behind, her nose assaulted by a smell like none before—the kind only experienced when you haven't showered in months. They heard a faint voice sobbing and slowly made out the silhouette of a child freezing in fear. The girls froze too; if they died here, nobody would know what happened. As the lighting improved, Katie suddenly recognised her as Nandita and rushed forward to hug her tightly. Mandy stayed back, quietly observing their reunion.

Once they had reunited, Katie felt they needed to leave quickly, or else risk being left behind.

"We need to go back now! We don't have much time and we will leave with you!" she declared, certain that they all had to depart together.

Mandy assisted Nandita as she struggled to stand in the dismal prison cell she had been confined in for so long. Though she was feeble, Nandita was determined to escape and not allow her circumstance to be her undoing.

Ten

The Graveyard Letters

Mandy's brows furrowed in confusion as she tried to make sense of what was happening.

"Wait, I don't want to ruin this reunion, but how can you even see Katie? I thought I was the only one that could see her." Her voice was laced with perplexity.

Nandita let out a heavy sigh, closing her eyes for a moment before reopening them.

"Well, when we were held captive in this cage-" she gestured towards the rusted metal structure behind them, "the man kept us fed, clothed, and so on. But one day, Katie got angry with him and he took her out of our cage for a while. When he came back, she was dead."

Mandy's hand flew up to her mouth in horror as realization dawned on her. The bones they had found belonged to Katie.

"I think it must have something to do with why I can still see her," Nandita continued softly, her gaze fixed firmly on the ground below their feet.

"Maybe it's some kind of spiritual thing because I was so close to her like you are, Mandy, but I'm not sure." She paused for a moment before looking up at Mandy once again, a pensive expression etched onto her features.

Both girls stood there in silence for a few moments, staring down at the remains of their friend. Nandita's words hung heavily between them like an invisible shroud.

"I have a feeling that this is why I can still see her," Nandita finally said, breaking the silence.

The distant sound of leaves rustling in the wind was the only response they received as they continued to stare down at the bones of their friend, contemplating what had happened all those years ago.

The hall was dark and dank; the smell of mildew and human decay was pervasive in the air. It smelt like death and decay, but a worse fate was in store. Mandy felt her stomach twist and knot up as she looked at what awaited them - a series of cages with iron bars. Each of the cages contained a child that they used for experiments, all under fifteen years old, except for one - a young man who stumbled around blindly like an animal trying to find something to eat or drink. The man couldn't talk properly, nor could he do anything besides grunt and scratch his head. Nandita's face brightened with excitement; she had not been outside in so long; she didn't know what the world outside looked like anymore. She tried to turn to Mandy to speak, but Mandy lifted her hand up to shush her. What if someone happened to hear? What if we get caught? Mandy thought with dread; she has an inkling of an idea who it might be.

Once they had reached the top of the stairs, Mandy and Katie waited for Nandita to reveal her true desires. They wanted this moment to be special for Nandita as she opened the lid. With delicate arms, Nandita slowly lifted it open, looking fragile compared to her surroundings. She was the first to step out, her hair blowing in the summers wind like leaves on a warm wintery night. As they walked further into the field, Nandita felt something that everyone should feel - it was comparable to finding a beloved toy from years ago. Her excitement spread to all three of them as they ran across the lush grass. Heading back towards their destination, they knew there wasn't much time left, but most importantly, they wanted Nandita to experience what it was like to be a normal child again. Hand in hand, they prepared for their teleportation.

As soon as they appeared in Mandy's room, Nandita started twirling around in delight, elated about having been so free, running and feeling the breeze on her entire body. Suddenly she stopped spinning when she realized one of her dearest friends had disappeared without a trace.

Katy found herself back in the graveyard, unable to move. Her legs were bound tightly, and she struggled to free herself from a heavy cloth case that had trapped her. She called out for help, but her voice was muffled by the cold dirt and grass that pressed against her cheek.

As she looked ahead, a figure was heading towards her. He moved slowly across the pavement, his strides long and drawn out with each step. His skin was ghostly pale and un-healthy-looking, like that of someone recently returned from a harrowing battle. His eyes were menacing and wicked, like that of a beast sizing up its prey before it pounced. Katy rec-ognized him, though she couldn't remember from where.

"What the hell is going on?" screamed Katie, her voice echoing off the walls as she took in her strange surround-ings. Her heart sank as memories of being forcefully taken flooded back.

"That's right! I'm Anthony, and I maintain these grounds. You are supposed to be six feet underground, but I can't put you there without consequences," Anthony stammered nervously. He could feel the danger radiating from Katie's quivering frame and knew he had to act quickly.

"You have my word that I will answer your questions and get help if needed."

The figure before her seemed harmless at first, but now Katie realized he was a predator masquerading under false colours. His malignant intentions were clear.

Eleven

The Courage

As the two of them searched Mandy's room for Katie, they realized that she had probably teleported into the wrong place.

"She could be anywhere in the world by now!" Mandy fretted.

Nandita agreed; it seemed like their only option was to hope that Katie would somehow manage to teleport back or reach out to them psychically. Though Mandy was just a human and neither of them knew where exactly Katie was, they braced themselves for the difficult task before them—to confront Mandy's grandparents about all the wrongs they'd done. The stairs seemed to lead toward an awful moment, but they treaded on reluctantly. This time, the floor didn't creak under their steps, but Mandy's sweat did instead as they reached the door. She thought hard about what she should say to them, but her mind went blank. She had no idea what to do and Nandita didn't either.

Mandy had a crazy idea - they should restrain the victims and trap them in the basement, allowing them to experience being held captive and feeling scared. She went back into the depths of the basement to find some rope and duct tape, then returned to the upper level with Nandita.

As soon as the door creaked open, Mandy and her friend were assaulted by the sight of her grandparents' feet. The curtains were drawn back to let in a stream of blinding light that illuminated only the bottoms of their bodies.

Without warning, Nandita shouted out a monstrous "BOO!" causing her grandfather to jump in surprise, sending beads of sweat cascading down his aging face. Her grandmother was not so lucky; swooning to the side like a piece of meat on a hook. In a fit of depraved ecstasy, the two girls decided to take matters into their own hands and trap Mandy's unsuspecting grandparents in her basement.

With ropes bound tightly around their emaciated limbs, the old couple cried out with hollow screams as the cords bit painfully into their flesh. Grandma's skin began to bruise and blister under the cruel pressure of the girls' merciless knots. Nandita loomed over Mandy's Grandpa, whose eyes widened with terror at the sight of his would-be captors. His was the face she associated with years of captivity and torment - a wave of hatred emanating from within her as she slapped him hard across his wrinkled cheek. Grinning with wicked pleasure, she gazed down upon him with unspeakable contempt for all he had done.

As Mandy and her evil Grandparents advanced down the stairs, she shouted for them to halt. She peered over the top of the staircase into the basement, reliving memories of her grandmother's mistreatment - how life had been beat out of her and replaced by fear. Without hesitation, Mandy thrusted her grandmother downwards, causing her to plunge into the abyss with a scream muffled by the tape over her mouth. Her grandfather shrieked in despair at the sight of his wife plummeting away from him, disappearing through the darkness below.

Mandy glared at her grandfather in disbelief. How could this be the same man who had provided her with nourishment when she was young and disregarded his wife's demands to care for her? In that moment, Mandy realised it was only for his own financial gain; the depth of sadness returned to her chest. Even though she loathed him, she still felt sympathy for him. Before Mandy could dwell on the thought further, Nandita pushed him down the stairs without a second thought. He was a predator and a murderer, thus deserving of death.

The thin, grey light struggled to penetrate the dark basement through a crack at the bottom of the door. It cast ghostly shadows across the stones, whispering in the wind like a siren's song. The two young girls paused at the threshold, feeling a sudden wave of anxiety and anticipation sweep over them. Hearing the two elderly voice calling from within with a renewed youthfulness and strength, they locked eyes for one moment, both knowing what had to be done. With courage and determination radiating between them, they descended into the darkness, preparing themselves for any challenge that might await them.

Twelve

The Realization

Katie's wrath was palpable as she fumed, "I don't care about those letters--what I do care about is why you kidnapped me!"

"Just relax," Anthony said, trying to keep his own anger in check.

"I'm not concerned with what happened to you; rather, what I want to know is why your grave isn't where it should be. But I can't risk my job by letting someone escape their death like this." He shuddered at the thought.

The two glared at each other as if they were ready to go to war. Then the blue door with a golden knob opened behind Anthony and his friend emerged. He was dressed in dark overalls and black trousers, muddy boots, and a bright pink t-shirt with colourful spots that almost looked like a rainbow. His skin was chocolate brown and he had orangey red hair knitted into dreads, and he was built strong like a hunter and had an orange moustache.

"What's going on here? Why is this young girl in the circle of death?" Jack asked, his eyes wide with amazement. Anthony shifted uncomfortably and mumbled an apology. They both looked at Jack like he was crazy, and Jack responded by shaking his head in disbelief and twirling his orange dreads.

"Hey, Jack," said Anthony sadly, pointing at Katie.

"I'm sorry; this ghost won't go back to her grave."

Katie spoke up. "Sir, I don't know why I'm here, but I don't think he has the right to kidnap me like this! We were so close to figuring it out, then he stops me for no reason and I can't even use my powers in this stupid circle!"

Jack held up his hands in surrender. "Okay, okay, now I understand the situation. Anthony, you should try talking to the ghost before getting angry—would you be happy if someone magically kidnapped you while you were trying to do something important?"

Anthony shook his head.

"No, no I wouldn't."

He turned to Katie. "And what did you say your name was?"

"Katie," she replied with a scowl at Anthony. "Thank you for being polite enough to ask, unlike some people."

"Okay, Katie, tell me how it would feel if someone completely disregarded your efforts and instead screamed at you?" asked the kind giant.

"I wouldn't like that very much..." replied Katie.

"Ahh! See, now: empathy! You know how the other person is feeling and why they are reacting this way. No more screaming - I can finally take my nap," said Jack in a grumpy old man voice.

"Yeah, I understand why you were so angry and I'm really sorry for overreacting." apologized Katie.

"Same here. It's my fault too; I should've thought about your situation before flying off the handle. I now understand not all ghosts want revenge or to cause harm; forgive me," Anthony looked into Katie's eyes with sincerity.

No longer adversaries, but allies - Anthony knew what had to be done about the grave problem he faced and had a plan forming in his head.

"Alright spirit; now that we both get each other, tell me what it is you have to do."

Katie nodded, as she tried to explain in detail everything that had taken place over the past few hours.

Anthony pursed his lips and lifted his eyebrows,

"Right then…explain that to me again." Katie rolled her eyes and sighed,

"This is the last time I will repeat myself, okay, so….. I met my friend Mandy at the graveyard you're working in. And then we went to her grandparents basement where I tried to find out how I died."

Anthony nodded as he sipped his tea. He choked on a laugh that erupted and exclaimed,

"Oh my goodness gracious! That was an awesome twist, wasn't it?"

Watching Anthony's body language as he foolishly joked around several times, but at the same time watching him get nervous, Katie looked on. Anthony spat out tea while exclaiming,

"Oh my, how do you come up with this stuff?!"

Katie scoffed incredulously, completely taken off guard by what she was hearing from Anthony,

"What! Do you not care about the fact that I died because of an old creepy man?! Or the fact that I'm a human being who might have wanted to live and didn't get the choice like all of us do every day?!"

Anthony shrugged without any emotion in his eyes and answered frankly in a monotone voice,

"Actually…no. You aren't human now so there's nothing for me to be concerned about."

Katie looked younger than she really was when she got angry and turned red in her face as she yelled at him, "I can't believe I actually wanted to be friends with someone so heartless…. So black-hearted…. A sociopath!"

Anthony's grin disappeared from his face as he regarded the girl before him.

"What about that look you gave me when your friend came in?"

Katie looked away in embarrassment and anger. Her recent realization was merely an angry thought form, but it was all she had left. Anthony gritted his teeth and placed his hands on her shoulders. His brute strength dug into her muscles like a pile driver. Katie wanted to step back but couldn't budge even an inch with the iron-like grip he had on her. She tried to pry herself free, but he held on even tighter.

"I was only doing it for him, in fact I don't even care about that guy, He's just a kind lowlife who always thinks he can solve every problem," he said as he glanced over at the door.

"You know, if I really cared about you, I might have let you go. But now…" He laced his fingers together around her neck and squeezed like a vice grip until his knuckles turned white and veins protruded from underneath his pale skin.

Panic surged through her veins as she glanced around, trying to decipher if she was going to be stuck in the room forever and die all over again. She spotted a small table with a computer on top, as well as a picture frame on its side. Meanwhile, Anthony planned her fate behind her. With fear stirring in her chest, she leaned forward and tried to get a better view of the frame. As soon as she took in the image of two parents and one child (whose faces were barely visible), her heart started beating fast and rage grew within her. Then, Anthony stepped closer with a sickeningly happy grin on his face.

"Oh… what are you looking at? Katie, isn't it?" he laughed.

Katie tensed up, worried this might be the last thing she would ever hear. "W-w…who are those people?" Katie stuttered out.

"I suppose I may as well tell you since you'll never escape from here," Anthony roared menacingly. "That's me and my parents when I was eight; I remember it like it was only yesterday," he said, walking towards the photo and grabbing it off the frame. He proceeded towards Katie, raising the image above his head before asking, "Do you recognise these faces?"

Katie let out an audible gasp as she noticed the resemblance between him and the figures on the page. "I know! They look just like me, don't they?" Anthony asked rhetorically while holding up the photograph for comparison.

"Everyone said I inherited my father's cheekbones, but then - "

"NO!" Katie gasped, "That – that's the man who killed me? He's your f - father!?"

Anthony let out a loud laugh. "I guess I shouldn't be too surprised; you were the one they killed on January second, right?"

"Y – yes." Katie felt all her hairs stand on end.

"Well, good thing I got here when I did, because now you can never reveal that to anyone." Anthony said before sitting down and declaring "Let the ritual begin!"

Katie screamed in horror, as he quickly lit a candle and began waving it around while speaking in a language Katie couldn't understand - it sounded French, but she had been home-schooled so she couldn't tell for sure. He turned up some hip hop music to muffle her screams. She could feel her strength slowly draining away.

"Please! STOP!" Katie screeched, but Anthony was too busy and didn't hear her. It seemed like she was vanishing right before her own eyes; she felt herself slipping away towards the Afterlife. With one last cry for help, Jack rushed in; red eyed from being woken up by Katie's screams and clutching a muddy shovel in his hands. Her eyes widened as he ran towards Anthony who was too absorbed in the music to even notice him coming. Jack swung with full force, making Anthony fall to the ground with the candle beside him causing him to scream in pain before Jack hit him once more. Katie looked on in shock.

"Don't worry," Jack said softly, "He's not dead – just knocked out."

Katie stepped down from the stone circle and stood over Anthony. His head was bruised and bloody—and she would have felt sorry for him, if it weren't for the fact he tried to kill her.

"Okay," she mumbled.

Jack kicked away the circle, creating a gap between Katie and the wounded man.

"I can't stand the sight of blood," Katie sighed.

"'I bet you can't,'" Jack said with a smile, "Now you need to go back to your friends, as you don't have much time left." He looked saddened by this thought.

"But what about?" Katie began.

"I'll take care of him… I assure you - I've done this before." He gave her a knowing wink.

"Okay.. I'll go, why did you help me?"

"Why wouldn't I? I understand that beneath that ghostly form lies a human being - even if he doesn't realise it himself." Jack cast an expression of disappointment in Anthony's direction.

"NOW GO!" Jack ordered pointing outside. Katie winced at the sound his voice made, but she followed his orders anyway.

Thirteen

The Journey

Mandy and Nandita were in the basement with her grandparents, who were confined and injured. The girls wanted to know what had happened, so Nandita asked,

"How many were there?" Mandy's grandfather remained silent for a few moments before replying,

"Too numerous to count." She continued to interrogate him, demanding,

"Where are their bodies? Where did you bury them?"

He shook his head again and mouthed his answer, "In the backyard, there are hundreds of graves."

The girls stood speechless, their faces reflecting shock at what they were hearing.

Mandy's words lingered in the air as what felt like a lifetime passed while she posed the question she'd been dying to ask.

Mandy glared at her grandparents, asking them why they had killed her parents. As she removed the tape from her grandmother's mouth, she could see the guilt in their eyes.

"It was an accident," said her grandmother meekly. "Lies!" shouted Mandy. "You killed them; I saw you poison them! Now tell me the truth or I will never let you out of this room!"
Her grandmother trembled as she spoke.

"YES, YES I DID IT. Your mother didn't care for you anyways." Out of anger Mandy kicked a chair that her grandmother was sitting on, causing her to tumble to the ground. Her grandfather cried out for her to stop.

"Look," he said, "your parents found out about what we were doing and your grandmother wouldn't listen--she thought they would go to the police!"

"What did my parents find out? Mandy inquired.

"Everything", he replied. "They knew that we were kidnapping children, selling them, and killing them. She wanted us to turn ourselves in, but we couldn't; our addiction was too powerful. You don't understand how it feels to have an uncontrollable urge to kill", he said exasperatedly.

"So you're telling me that you've been murdering kids for years and killed my parents when they found out about your addiction? And now here you are, with no remorse what-soever? I can't believe that I used to love you", whispered Mandy.

"Look please try to understand, we just couldn't stop there was no way around it", he continued weakly.

Mandy muttered the words, "If your right hand causes you to sin, cut it off and throw it away," as she clutched her grandfather's frail body. Her hands trembled as she slowly reached into her pocket and pulled out a knife. She froze in place for a few seconds, unable to bring herself to carry out the act that her faith required of her. Suddenly rage over-came her and with one quick motion, she spun around and began thrusting the blade into his body repeatedly. Every stab was accompanied by her grandfather's screams for mercy, yet Mandy could not stop.

Nandita watched in silence as the oppressive atmosphere filled the room. Mandy's grandmother cried for help but fell upon deaf ears as Mandy continued to plunge a knife back and forth into her grandfather's body, her face twisted into a grotesque mask of rage like that of a tiger lunging at its prey. Nandita inched towards her, gently placing her hand on Mandy's shoulder as she reminded her she needed to snap out of it; that it was okay to let go. Slowly, Mandy complied, allowing Nandita to take the bloody weapon away from her, still dripping with her grandfather's blood.

Meanwhile, Mandy's grandma begged her husband for a response from the basement. She shouted his name to no avail. It was the first time Karen ever felt so powerless.

Gasping for air, Mandy sank to the floor and glared at her grandfather. Unbidden memories of her mother came flooding back, her earrings twinkling in the sunlight; her warm and inviting smile; her deep green eyes blinking innocently; that signature red lipstick; the pretty pink blush she'd always wear on her cheeks. Her father sat in the driver's seat singing and bopping to the music, his imposing yet comforting presence taking over the car. At that moment, she realised maybe it would be best if she left this world, so she could join her parents once again in the afterlife.

As she sat and pondered her existence, Mandy failed to notice Nandita approaching her until the latter sat down beside her. At that moment, Katie teleported through the wall and was stunned by what she saw before her. "What happened?" asked Katy in disbelief, staring at Mandy's bloodied form and her grandfather lying on the ground, bleeding out. Silence hung heavy in the room until Karen screamed, "She killed him! She killed my husband!" Katie knelt down next to Mandy and asked if she was okay.

Without answering, Mandy said, "I'm ready to go home;

this world is not for me." Confused, Katie pressed for more information, but all Mandy wanted was to be reunited with her family. As Karen lay on the ground slogging over like a fat cow, trying to piece together what was happening, Mandy and Nandita spoke quietly amongst themselves. A wave of panic washed over Karen as she struggled to turn around with her hands bound behind her back.

As a loud bang echoed through the house, Nandita and Mandy felt fear course through their veins.

"Mum, dad!" shouted the booming voice upstairs, sending shockwaves through them that could not be contained.

"We have to go now, Mandy; I need to tell you something and get you away from here before something else happens,"

Katie pleaded, her eyes begging for understanding.

Mandy was torn between leaving and staying—she had just stabbed her grandfather moments ago. But a somber reality settled in as she saw the urgency in Katie's gaze: they had no choice but to flee.

"Help me, Anthony! Please!" Karen screamed, as Katie grabbed each of their hands to teleport away. The unknown awaited them as they were submerged in darkness; Karen was petrified of what lay ahead.

Fourteen

The Pain

"Mum! Dad! Where are you?!" Anthony shouted out loud.

"I'm in here!" Karen screamed from behind the door.

Anthony yanked at the door handle, trying desperately to get inside the basement room. As soon as he opened it, he was greeted with an unbelievable sight: his mother Karen lay tied up on the cold, hard ground, her hands and feet bound while tears streamed down her face.

"Are you okay mother?" He rushed over to untie her.

"I'm just fine sweetie, but your father-" She stopped herself mid-sentence, her voice thick with emotion. When Anthony looked down at his father's body lying on the floor, his eyes widened in shock. There was blood pooling around him and his mouth hung open lifelessly. He couldn't detect a pulse. Anthony held his father close and cried helplessly.

"Who did this mum, NOOOOO! why, how did this happen"? He yelled out in distress.

"Don't cry baby! I'm sure he's alright… but we might need to get him to the hospital," Karen said as she fought back tears. She looked at her husband's lifeless body and felt her heart break into two.

"We have to go Anthony; we have to pack and leave right now".

Anthony stood up, his clothing now covered in blood. He looked to his mother with confusion.

"But where, where will we go, what is going on? Look mother something happened at the graveyard today, I, I can't explain it but, I think one of the girls is back to hurt us."

Karen stared back at her son, she had known this day would come eventually; it was only a matter of when.

"Let's go" she shouted, as the two hurried upstairs to gather their belongings.

Fifteen

Danger Awaits

When the trio materialized in the front garden, Katie crumpled to the ground. She lay there, motionless and gasping for breath, so pale her blue veins were visible under her skin. Mandy and Nandita crouched beside her, terrified she might be dead. They drew back, hands covering their mouths, as Katie rolled over onto her side and coughed. She still breathed but looked weak.

"Something happened," Mandy said softly to Nandita. "We must go inside."

Katie trembled as she spoke, her voice rasping with anguish and fear.

"No!" she cried out, her body wracked with sobs,

"We can't go back in there! I know what's been going on

- it was your family that's been doing this- taking innocent kids and selling their organs on the black market. Hundreds of children gone without a trace... Your grandparents were mass murderers!" Her words hung heavy in the air as she collapsed onto the forgotten grass, weeping uncontrollably.

Mandy's voice trembled with a mix of fury and bewilderment. "Yes, I know," she said in a low, strained voice that seemed to suggest she was barely keeping it together.

"They finally confessed - they were the ones responsible for all these missing children." She paused and took a deep breath as if to calm herself down but then continued in a wavering tone, "I just can't believe that someone I trusted could do something so heinous."

From her quivering lips and tearful eyes, it was clear that Mandy was struggling to reconcile the image of the person she once knew with this new revelation. For a long moment, there was silence as they both tried to absorb the weight of what was being said.

She felt torn between the two worlds that threatened to consume her. On one hand, she wanted justice for her beloved's death, yet on the other, she desperately hoped and prayed for some kind of reprieve.

"Why did they let me live when they took away my reason for living?" She breathed in deep, letting out a shuddering sigh as the conflicting emotions washed over her.

Katie replied, "Because your parents had life insurance money left for you. Once you turned 18 and claimed it, that's when they planned to murder you too. That's why they abused you but not enough to take your life."

Realization dawned on Mandy's face as she sighed in disbelief.

"I can't believe I didn't see this from the beginning—how could I have been so stupid?"

Katie reassured her gently, "It wasn't your fault, Mandy. You can't blame yourself for this."

Katie was getting desperate as she pleaded with Mandy to leave.

"We need to go now," she repeated, her voice getting urgent. "I can feel my strength slipping away from me as each second passes. We have to get to the graveyard; I know someone there who can help us."

Mandy began to walk around in circles, trying desperately to weigh her options. She knew that they needed to act fast if Katie had any hope of surviving, but she couldn't shake the feeling that they had to report what her grandparents had done - that there could be more innocent children out there who needed their help. Finally, she nodded and reluctantly agreed.

"Okay, let's go," she replied hesitantly. "But first, I have to stop at the police station and tell them everything my grandparents were doing."

"Alright, here's the plan," Nandita began, her voice hushed but insistent. The urgency of their situation weighed heavily on them all. She glanced at each member of their small group before continuing. "We'll have to divide and conquer if we want any chance of saving Katie."

Mandy nodded in agreement while Katie chewed nervously on her bottom lip.

"Mandy, you dash to the police station as fast as you can while I help Katie get to the graveyard quickly. If we don't make it there in time," she grimaced at the thought, "she may vanish without a trace and you know what that could mean."

The last thing they wanted was for anything bad to happen. But with so much at stake, they had no choice but to take the risk. Sweat prickled on their brows and their hearts pounded hard against their chests as they tried to split up and hurry off towards their respective destinations.

Katie felt the ground shift beneath her as she was lifted up by the arms of her friends, but before they could get far, a deafening gunshot ripped through the air. In the distance, a red truck was looming closer and closer, until they could make out Mandy's grandmother and Anthony in the driver and passenger seat, with a rifle pointed directly at them. Another shot echoed out as Anthony tugged at the trigger and everyone screamed, the bullet whizzing past Mandy's ear, ringing in her ears. She watched it whiz by, a fury of red and black traveling at a lightning speed.

Katie was faced with a gun pointing directly at her. She let out an ear-piercing scream as the bullet flew past her face, bringing with it the smell of burned powder and smoke. All of their pounding hearts seemed to resonate within her chest.

Mandy's grandmother slowly stepped out of the car, her body almost disobeying her orders. The bright parking lot lights illuminated the cracked asphalt and cast long, looming shadows that surrounded her. She tightened her grip on the short-barrelled pump action shotgun as the car door hinges screeched in protest, and she flinched at the sound before mustering enough courage to continue forward.

"We must go now, Mandy. It's your grandmother and Anthony; they will kill us if we don't," Nandita said frantically as she tried to stand up.

"Okay guys, you go ahead of me. I'll meet you at the cemetery after I finish my business at the police station."

They all attempted to embrace each other before another gunshot made them scatter for cover, Mandy running off into the distance while Katie and Nandita made a bee-line for the graveyard.

"Come on, Katie! You have to go now!" Nandita shouted.

"I... I don't think so. I'm too weak," Katie replied.

"Alright then, what about teleportation? Can you do that?" Nandita asked.

"No, unfortunately not," Katie said. "My body is too drained."

Nandita grabbed onto Katie's frail frame and ran off into the woods. The leaves and brush crunch under their feet with every step. The wind was supernaturally loud and the trees creaked as their branches were pushed out of the way by the speeding bullet, the sound of the footsteps of running travel a hollow echo as they rushed across the open field. Nandita looked back to catch a glimpse of Anthony and his mother, who had split up in pursuit. Without a doubt, Anthony had murder in his eyes as he sprinted after them.

As they kept running away for safety, Nandita concealed Katie's body in a pile of foliage.

"Be quiet and don't make a sound," Nandita warned her before adding: "I'll come back for you I promised." She tucked the leaves around Katie tenderly before taking off into the night.

Anthony's rage-fuelled his thunderous steps as he stalked

through the night, his gun clutched in a tight grip. His acute senses searching the choking darkness for Nandita as he followed her scent. A sliver of pale moonlight revealed her silhouette ahead of him and without a second thought, he fired multiple shots in succession like lightning cracking across a starless sky. One bullet caught her in the thigh causing agony to rip through her veins and she fell to the ground with a scream. He advanced on her slowly, an evil grin plastered on his face as if drawn there by malicious intent, relishing in his command over her. With eyes glowing with anger and hate, he stared down at her trembling form while beads of sweat rolled down her pale skin and into her wide eyes. Dropping to one knee beside her, he placed the cold barrel of the gun against her forehead, delighting in the fear that shone from her deep brown gaze.

Fury surged through his veins as he cocked the gun and stared down at her. "You should have never ventured out here," he spat, "You foolish girl! Now I will make sure you stay locked away where you belong!" As he yelled, his finger slowly tightened around the trigger.

Nandita froze in shock as her eyes locked onto the gun, coming face-to-face with death once again. The acrid smell of gunpowder permeated the air, assaulting her senses and reminding her that lives were lost here. Fear pulsed through her veins like electric currents, and she realized the gun was still loaded and ready to fire.

Memories of her childhood when she was full of joy

rushed back to her. She remembered what it felt like before they snatched her away from her beloved family and friends. This time around, she was determined not to let that happen again. Before he could pull the trigger, Nandita lunged forward and plunged her sharp blade deep into his heart, twisting it mercilessly. "You should have been left to die in that crib," she snarled, her eyes burning with fury as they bore into his own. His gun clattered to the ground from limp fingers and he slumped back, a look of shock and surprise still frozen upon his face.

She carefully backed up and crawled over to a nearby tree, studying his corpse in silent shock. Wounded by a bullet meant for her, she painfully used the trunk of the tree to stand. The leaves on the nearby trees rustled in the breeze that swept past her. The gun on the ground glistened in the sunlight, and the man's open eyes stared at the heavens.

The bullet's entry point was hidden by her clothes, but she could feel the warm blood trickling down to her thigh. Nandita bit her lip and tried not to cry out, knowing that the last thing Katie needed to see was her friend suffering.

Her leg was soaked with blood, a dark crimson blemish against the pristine green leaf's. Then, with one last limping effort, she made her way back to where she had hidden Katie for protection. She trudged through the darkness, her journey seemingly never ending as she walked closer to Katie. She hopped with impatience and growing anxiety, her feet almost a blur as each second felt like an eternity. As she arrived, Katie looked up at her friend with a weak smile.

"You have done your part, my dear," said Katie, her voice echoing with a deafening power. As she touched Nandita's arm, the young girl felt as if a cosmic current of energy was passing through their hands and into her soul. Katie could feel her strength slowly returning to her body, a surge so powerful that the air around them crackled with electricity.

"Let us go," Katie's voice was low and full of bliss. "Take me away from this horrid place and abandon him here in this abyss of misery to rot for all eternity!"

Without another word, they twisted through the air, soaring above the trees until the graveyard appeared below them. With one final glance back at Anthony, they vanished into the night, leaving him behind in the cursed forest.

Sixteen

The Fight for Survival

Mandy sprinted recklessly through the woods, bolting past tree trunks and leaping over roots. She was almost there. If she could make it to the police station before her grandmother caught up with her, everything would be okay. But then a deafening gunshot filled the air, followed by searing pain as hot lead tore into her body. Mandy screamed as she crashed to the ground, feeling something warm trickle down her face and onto her hands. She touched her ears and gasped when they came away reddened with blood. Desperately she scrambled for cover behind a large tree trunk, yanking out her phone in one hand and frantically dialling the police in the other. With muffled words she spoke urgently into the receiver, conveying all that had happened before time ran out.

Mandy screamed, a desperate plea for help that pierced through the night air.

"My name is Mandy and I'm in danger! My grandparents —they are serial killers and have buried children's bodies all over the house. If you don't come now, they will kill me!"

The police officer's voice quivered as he struggled to comprehend the horror of her words.

"Ma'am, please tell me where you are right away. I'll send someone out to you immediately."

Mandy's voice trembled as she spoke into the phone,

"Someone needs to come quickly. I live at 110 Brighton ro...".

Suddenly, her words were cut off by a chilling sight - her grandmother standing before her with a shotgun in hand, towering over Mandy like some sort of ominous-spectre. The gnarled old hands held the gun so tightly that it seemed an extension of her body, and Mandy couldn't tell if the weapon was there for protection or something far more sinister.

For a moment, the air around them seemed to thicken with palpable tension as Mandy struggled to understand what was happening. Was this really her beloved grandmother? Or had something taken hold of her, twisting her into a monster?

As if sensing Mandy's fear and confusion, the old woman slowly levelled the shotgun directly at Mandy's heart. And in that instant, everything became painfully clear - the only thing that awaited Mandy was death.

Mandy heard the loud bang of the rifle and felt a sharp agonizing pain in her forehead. She collapsed into a pile of decaying leaves, her warm tears seeping from her ears as blood trickled down her cheeks. Her grandmother dropped the gun barrel and grabbed Mandy's hair at the nape of her neck with one hand while using her other to land both knees into the young girl's kidney area. Instinctively, Mandy's hands went up to shield her face as her grandmother flung the phone across it. The force knocked out the fragile girl before she could even open her swollen eyes, leaving her motionless with the phone below her.

Seventeen

The Last Known Victim

Mandy stirred awake in the cold, dark chamber. She tried to move her arms and legs but was bound to a chair which held her captive. Blood trickled down her damaged face, and she could feel it oozing from where she had been struck; one eye was swollen so tightly shut that she wondered if she would ever see out of it again. The stench of human suffering filled the room like a miasma, like a sickening fog emanating from the wall-to-wall bodies encircling them on all sides. Memories of her grandmother's menacing gaze crept into Mandy's mind as she looked around the death chamber for the first time since being captured, and finally realized where she was: the same cell in which Nandita and Katy had been held captive. Terror flooded her veins like liquid fire as she surveyed the bedroom of horrific tools - sharp blades, loaded firearms, heavy ropes, deflated body bags - the reek of death was suffocating. Every sickening object seemed to be fated for the innocent children's bodies, for cutting and harvesting their organs in a silent massacre.

Mandy's grandmother sneered at her maliciously, her words dripping with scorn. Without warning she dashed a bucket of frigid water over Mandy's head, leaving her shivering in the cold.

"I was going to let you live until you turned eighteen," the old woman spat. "I had planned it all out so carefully! But you had to meddle and destroy all of my hard work. You even stole away the one person I ever truly loved." She finished her speech by winding back her arm and striking Mandy viciously in the stomach. Blood exploded from Mandy's lips as she crumpled to the ground, sobbing silently beneath the oppressive weight of her grandmother's cruelty.

"I loved Earl so much, he was my everything," she said as memories from her life with her husband came flooding back. She continued in a reverie-like state. "He was my best friend. We met when we were both teenagers in high school, he pursued me, not the other way around. His family had money and I didn't have anyone, when I was sixteen I was homeless but he took me in. My parents never paid attention to me; Earl was all I had. He recognized that I had anger issues and knew what I needed to do to release it. My life changed when I was eighteen. I was in a bar and a man tried to approach me, but after I rebuffed him, he punched me in the face so hard that my head knocked into the counter behind me and my vision blurred. Earl stepped up to defend me. He walked over to the drunkard and stood in front of him with his large frame like a wall of muscle, effectively stopping the man from coming any closer. My rescuer's dark eyes glinted as he stared down at the other man. We left that day, and Earl nursed my bruised cheek once we'd arrived home; it wasn't in his nature to be violent—but as a woman, it means so much when your partner is willing to defend you". She then lit a cigarette and exhaled the smoke into the air.

"As we watched the news in our old trailer, a body was reported. It had been beaten and burned until it became un-recognizable, tortured for days before anyone could identify it. I glanced up at Earl in horror, not wanting to believe what I saw. Without saying a word his face revealed that he would do anything to keep me safe." Standing with sudden purpose, she made her way over to the weapons table and picked up a gun. She marched back to her seat with profound determina-tion, taking slow drags from her cigarette as it burned down to its end.

"After that fateful night, bloodthirsty and desperate, we sought out more victims. We shifted our sights to innocent children, the perfect prey to meet our needs; no one would miss them or come looking for them, I mean why would they, my parents didn't want me, all they wanted was to drink and take drugs, all parents were the same. Anyway it was easy money, kidnapping kids and selling their organs, or so it seemed. But then Earl cheated on me with your mother's mother. She was scraggly and plain compared to my beauty; why did he want her? I despised your mother from the day she arrived with her soft voice and overall dullness. She seemed to have it better than everyone else which only fuelled my burning hatred for her. With every glance Earl gave her, I felt as if he loved her more than me—fuelling my jealousy and rage into a blazing inferno.

When your mother discovered what we had done, I knew I had to end it. She had become privy to too much information, and it seems like you now know too much" she said with a cold voice before shooting Mandy in the gut.

Mandy's vision faded in and out as the whites of her eyes receded. Her heart raced and her breath quickened, yet she was too numb to move. Her eyelids closed under their own weight until there remained only a pinhole through which light shone brightly. She could sense that consciousness was slipping away from her. As she resigned herself to the inevitable, Mandy saw a bright, sunset glow.

She stumbled upon a breath-taking landscape, the air heavy with the pungent scent of rose petals and lemons, the smell of roses saturated the air, invigorating every cell in her body.

The sun shone so brightly that it made the trees sparkle as if they were encrusted in diamonds. Every blade of grass was alive with vibrant wildflowers, like an infinite number of jewels decorating the land. The leaves and flower petals are iridescent, like a kaleidoscope, and reflect the sun's rays in all directions. Their petals are large and full, each one a dazzling display, making the whole more beautiful than a single petal could ever be.

Two figures came into view from far away, and she focused all her energy onto them, desperate to make out who they were. Could it be Katy and Nandita? She ran towards them with a newfound strength, banishing all of her previous physical pain. As she drew nearer, she saw the most beautiful woman in the world. A vision of radiance, a goddess of beauty. A woman with long brown hair that glowed in the sunlight, her delicate cheeks flushed pink beneath her diamond earrings that twinkled in the warmth. Her dress was dazzling from afar. It was her mother! Her mother appeared before her, wearing a dazzling dress glittering with hundreds of tiny diamonds. Her dark brown hair writhed in the breeze like a forest fire, the waves like a raging river. Her lips were red as blood, and her eyes were filled with love and kindness. Tears immediately flooded down her face as she embraced her mother and felt her father's tender kiss on her forehead. Her mother looked deeply into her eyes and wiped away each tear with gentle hands.

Mandy's heart raced as she beheld the sight of her beloved parents. They were exactly as she remembered them, undiminished by time and pain. Her eyes drank in the sight of them until her vision grew blurry with tears of joy. With a sudden surge of emotion, Mandy flung herself towards them, desperate to feel their embrace once more.

"Mom! Dad! I've missed you so much!" she cried out.

In response, her mother enfolded her in an embrace that seemed to last an eternity, whispering gentle reassurances into her ear. Mandy melted into that hug, savouring every second of it like the sweetest honey. Despite all she'd been through, she knew beyond a doubt that she was finally home. It felt too wondrous to be real. And yet here it was—it felt like divine retribution for all the struggles she had faced on her journey.

"Darling, it's not time yet," Mandy's mother said as she planted a slow kiss on her cheeks. Her father took her hands and gave her a reassuring smile. As they prepared to leave, Mandy felt herself being pulled back into the present moment. She opened her eyes to find her grandmother standing over her.

Suddenly, Mandy's grandmother brandished a gun and pointed it right at her.

"Tell your parents I said go to hell," she snarled as she prepared to fire the last shot into Mandy's chest. Before she could pull the trigger, however, police officers crashed through the door shouting, "Drop the weapon now!" and tackling Mandy's grandmother to the ground.

Mandy lay on the ground, her body wracked with pain from a gunshot wound to her abdomen and covered in cuts from the restraints that had bound her to the chair. A police-woman ran to her side and gently untied the ropes while speaking comforting words of reassurance. The tape was carefully removed from Mandy's mouth. She groaned as it came off, sending an arrow of additional pain through her.

Eighteen

Freedom

As Mandy's body weakened, paramedics placed her on a stretcher. The basement was surrounded by police and health workers as they carefully wheeled her down the corridor away from the death chamber. In her semi-conscious state,

She caught sight of a chaotic scene unfolding before her, a flood of young, frightened faces peer out from under blankets that draped over their small bodies. Officers in uniform usher them away down a narrow corridor leading out of the basement.

Mandy caught sight of the little ones hiding under the blankets, peeking out at her, their eyes wide, faces etched with fear as they saw a woman being wheeled away. Some were in chains, others had cuffs on their wrists and ankles.

There were little girls but also little boys. Maybe they were brothers or sisters or close friends, or maybe even unrelated, but there was no time to think about that now, only to feel their shared terror as they were escorted out of the basement, a prison for children. The sight of a large, desperate crowd of children, some gangly adolescents, others still toddlers. The children whimpered and moaned, each one's sobs echoing in the basement.

A thick, white, bandage wrapped around her face that supported a plastic breathing tube.

Mandy's vision was blurred by her tears but she caught a glimpse of herself passing by the hatch of a police van. A wave of dizziness and pain washed over her as more ambulance arrived at the scene. She tried to push herself up, tried to sit up, but she was too weak.

Mandy felt like she was in an action-packed thriller as she made her way to the top of the garden to see the children being freed. Her heart raced in anticipation, wondering if they'd make it out unscathed. But then she saw that her grandmother was in handcuffs, her hands tightly bound behind her back, and the police were carefully escorting her into the back of their patrol car. The metallic click of the handcuffs echoed through the clearing as Mandy's grandmother shot her a withering glance, unable to comprehend what was happening. Mandy watched in shock, rooted to the spot as if she were watching a terrible accident unfold before her eyes.

As the sun began to rise Mandy could hear the birds chirping in the distance, a gentle breeze rustling the leaves on the trees. The police officers descended on the house like a horde of locusts, their blue sirens piercing through the silence of night. Neighbours slipped out from behind tightly shut doors, some in dressing gowns and others still in pyjamas as they emerged into the eerie morning light. The sound of screams mixed with the flashing lights, bouncing off the walls until it seemed like an unending chorus of terror had echoed to every corner of the neighbourhood, leaving stunned silence in its wake as more neighbours joined the crowd.

Nandita limped over to Mandy, her leg now bandaged, and gave her a huge smile.

"We did it, Mandy! We did it!" Nandita exclaimed.

Mandy blinked in disbelief, overwhelmed by the joy she felt but unable to express it due to the tube covering her mouth. She lifted one hand and removed the tube from her face.

"But how did this happen? My phone broke," Mandy said as she attempted to explain that she had tried to call the police but her grandmother had destroyed her phone.

"Shh, it's okay," Nandita whispered soothingly.

"I know you're struggling, Mandy. After we helped Katie cross over into the afterlife, I went to the police myself.

When we didn't see you at the graveyard, I knew that you needed help. That's why I made sure that every police and news outlet would be here today." Nandita hopped on one leg as she spoke, her eyes shining with pride and love for her friend. As they gently smiled at each other they both saw Katie walking towards them from a distance. Her blonde hair fluttered in the breeze, and she looked like an angel, a bright light radiating from her figure. It was almost like she had descended from the heavens—her hair shone like a halo around her head, making her skin look angelic. When she reached them, she embraced Nandita with a hug and bent down to kiss Mandy on her forehead, sending warm happiness shining in their heart like sunlight through clouds.

Katie's eyes shone like the sun, her voice bursting with joy as she exclaimed "Best friends forever". Mandy blinked back tears of sorrow and joy, her heart aching over letting her friend go, yet marvelling at the freedom that was now within her grasp. She didn't know how she would tell Katie's parents but knowing that her dear friend was now free of the chains of her past brought a newfound peace to Mandy's soul. Her smile broadened despite her sadness, celebrating in Katie's liberation.

A massive front garden stretched out in front of Katie. The grass was thick and green, and spirits rose up from it like weeds to greet her. As she walked into the field, the colours of their lives poured over her in an amber wave, obscure and indistinguishably bright. There were so many that it was hard to count. They all waved goodbye from far away before disappearing. All the spirit resembles a mirage, translucent and vibrating as they hover above ground. Without a corporeal form, their appearances remain fluid, shifting with the light and wind. They can be any age, race or gender. Some appear like apparitions, others look alive.

The birds chirped happily as they flew from tree to tree. They cawed and squawked loudly and obnoxiously, a joyous cacophony. The cool morning breeze shakes the trees and flowers as they sway to the mysterious song of the wind. A few minutes later, the ambulance drives into the driveway and a team of paramedics run out to prepare Mandy for transport.

Mandy and Nandita watched with awe as this mysterious event transpired. A few moments later they loaded Mandy into the ambulance, helping Nandita inside afterward. As they fastened her in, Nandita held her hands and asked jovially,

Nandita turned to Mandy, her eyes ablaze with anticipation.

"Well best friend, what next?" Her voice echoed in the silence between them like a beacon of hope, and Mandy's heart surged joyously within her chest knowing she now had a partner-in-arms for this wild journey called life. A wide grin spread across her face as the two embarked on their shared destiny.

THE END
AT LEAST FOR NOW……

www.ingramcontent.com/pod-product-compliance
Lightning Source LLC
Chambersburg PA
CBHW061221210726
48294CB00006B/1934